THE GREAT LABNE TRADE

Eman Saleh

Illustrated by Eilnaz Barmayeh

To my older brother, who taught me the importance of hard work. Thank you for having my back when I didn't wake up for my paper route. You had the better route anyways... :)

And to my dearest mother, who taught me the importance of sacrifice and believing in your children. No matter how wild and crazy our ideas were, you supported them. Thank you for supporting our dreams, one labne sandwich at a time. 🩶

"You're late for school! Don't forget your lunch," Mom cried.

Ahmed grabbed his bag and
peeked inside.

"Labne sandwiches? No, this just won't do. All the kids will laugh, and they will say, 'Ewww!' Can't I have a normal meal? P B and J would be ideal."

"Be proud of who you are, my dear. Now go to school and have no fear. One day you will appreciate how special you are. Stand tall, and don't let them make you feel small."

The next day at lunch, Ahmed pulled the labne out of his bag. His friends all asked, "What is that?" Then they sneered. "It's making us gag!"

Ahmed felt embarrassed, but he
remembered his mother's words.
I have to stand tall, he thought.
They are being absurd.

"You laugh now, but this sandwich is like no other. It's made from the best ingredients by my very own mother."

Josh chimed in. "Well, it does smell pretty good. Maybe you can split it with us? It'd be nice if you would."

The labne was split three ways, one piece for each friend.
They each took a bite, and it put the teasing to an end.

Alex squealed, "This is phenomenal! Something I've never tasted! Will you eat the rest? I don't want to see it wasted."

That was the start of the Great Labne Trade.

Ahmed's mother worked late each night to have the sandwiches made.

At first, he gave them away, but saw an opportunity flash before his eyes. *I can sell these to my friends,* he thought. *I wouldn't need to advertise.*

"Step right up!" he called. "Come one, come all.
25 cents a pop! They're selling quickly, don't stall."

The line started out small, but it quickly grew. It grew, and it grew,
and soon everyone knew ... about the little boy with the scrumptious
roll-ups. No one was safe from the labne, not even the grown-ups.

Ahmed became an overnight sensation, but made sure everyone received an invitation, to indulge in this delightful treat, even for those who had no money to eat.

Trading quickly became a way for folks to join in if they couldn't pay. Toys, baseball cards, anything would do, just as long as it was something valuable and new.

But soon, the demand was much too high. *I have to increase my prices,* he thought. *Nobody would bat an eye.* To anyone who questioned the rising costs, he justified it with the time he had to exhaust.

He went on to explain, "Folks, it's
simply a case of supply and demand.
I'm pretty much a household brand."

And he was right. The lines were out the door. Even with the up-charge, people were asking for more. They simply couldn't get enough, of the bread, tomatoes, and yogurt stuff.

Sure enough, cafeteria food became a thing of the past. *This is just a fad,* the lunch ladies thought. *This will not last.*

Boy were they wrong. Business
showed no signs of slowing down.

"How much longer can this go on?"
The lunch ladies all frowned.

Ahmed worried that his business would reach its peak. "I need something different, to attract more folks next week."

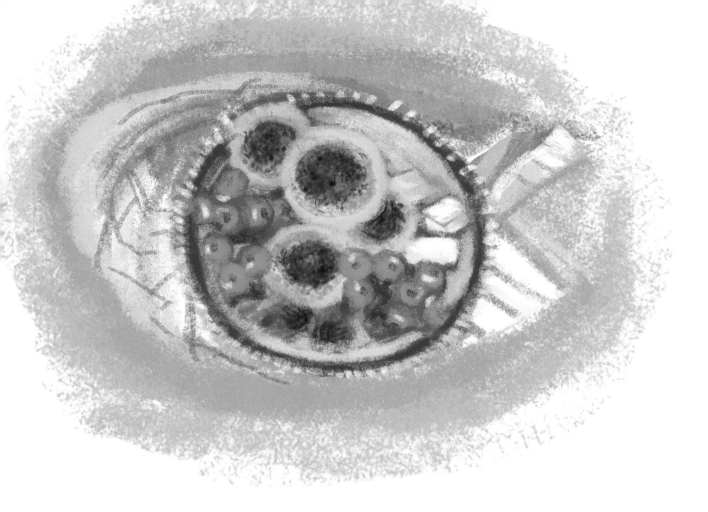

He brainstormed and thought and thought.
"I need a fresh taste, something tangy and new."

The lines continued to grow. People were coming and going at a steady flow.

They were eager to try the newest item
on the menu. Word continued to spread,
and his business grew, and it grew.

The lunch ladies became cross
and demanded change.

They had enough and marched to the principal, who was in close range.

The principal saw with his very own eyes, how the cafeteria
had transformed, and he heard the lunch ladies' cries.

"From now on, food is not to be sold or traded! This stops now!" the principal berated.

And just like that, the Great Labne Trade was done. No more sandwiches. No more lines. The lunch ladies won.

But fear not for Ahmed's fate. This was just the beginning, just a small taste.

You see, this boy grew older and smarter. He graduated with his business degree. He was a self starter.

Now whenever he feels unsure or doesn't know what to do,
he remembers his mother's words that always rang true.

His mother, the unsung hero who supported his dream. She worked tirelessly in the kitchen. They were a remarkable team.

The Great Labne Trade **may now be gone,**

but Ahmed's legacy and entrepreneurial spirit will always live on.

About the Author

Eman Saleh, author of *A Twin Tale*, resides in Michigan with her husband and four children. A former elementary and special education teacher, Eman uses her teaching experiences to help her craft her writing. She has a passion for education and owns and operates an early childhood education center.

Eman utilizes diverse characters to tell everyday stories. Eman believes it is important for all children to feel represented, something she was devoid of feeling growing up as an Arab American Muslim. "*The Great Labne Trade*" is inspired by the true story of her older brother's business ventures in the school cafeteria.

When she is not writing, she can be found reading, running, catching one her favorite Broadway shows, or enjoying a classic Disney movie. She is a self proclaimed child at heart!

All About Labne

What is Labne?

Labne is a thick, tangy, yogurt spread
commonly found in the Middle East.
It can be served as a spread to accompany
your breakfast, rolled into a sandwich,
used as a dip, and more!

How it's prepared

Labne is often paired with olive oil, zaa'tar,
or other fresh herbs, and fresh vegetables,
such as tomatoes, cucumbers, and fresh
mint.

Where I can get it?

You can find Labne in the refrigerated
aisle of many grocery stores, or you can
make it yourself!

Printed in the USA
CPSIA information can be obtained
at www.ICGtesting.com
LVHW061812020124
767832LV00021B/1239